HANNA-BARBERA
FLINTSTONES'
DOUBLE RUBBLE TROUBLE

One day Fred Flintstone arrived home from his job at the rock mine. He entered the house in his usual fashion, slamming the front door and shouting "Wilma! I'm home!" making such a racket that eleven slates fell off the roof, every dog in Bedrock began to howl, and pictures and mirrors fell off the walls.

At dinner, the first few minutes went by without any conversation. Finally, Fred looked at

Wilma and said, "Hey! You're kind of quiet tonight — something on your mind?"

Wilma replied with a sigh, "Well, sort of. It's all mixed up."

"What's all mixed up?" asked Fred.

"Betty Rubble." said Wilma.

"Betty Rubble's all mixed up?" asked Fred. "Why's that bothering **you**?"

"Oh, I'm mixed up, too!" Wilma answered.

"What are you both mixed up about?" Fred wanted to know.

"Well," Wilma said, "The department store was having a sale of washrags today, and —"

Fred interrupted. "Washrags? How can you get mixed up about washrags?"

"You **said** tell it from the beginning," replied Wilma. "Stop interrupting me or I'll just **never** get it straight!"

Fred said, "Go on. Holy

mackerel—a washrag mixup!"

"Anyhow," Wilma continued, "we went downtown and we each bought washrags. I didn't have the right change, so Betty loaned me fourteen cents to make it come out even. Or was it fifteen cents? Maybe I loaned **her** the fifteen cents-or fourteen cents. I guess that's when we started to get mixed up."

"I can tell you one thing for sure," Fred said, "You're starting to get **me** mixed up, too!"

"There's more," Wilma said. "By the time we finished with the washrags, and looked at some draperies and bed linens and a few more things, we were sort of thirsty, so we went to the drug store for a cool drink. That's where it got **really** mixed up!"

"In the **drug** store?" Fred yelled. "How'd you get mixed up in the drug store?"

"Don't **shout** so, Fred!" pleaded Wilma. "I have a bad headache already! Where was I? Oh—the drug store. Well—Betty treated me to a lemon soda."

"**That** sounds simple enough," Fred said..

"I suppose it was," sighed Wilma, "except that by that time **Betty** didn't have any change, so I paid for it! You see why I'm mixed up? I can't remember whether I owe Betty fourteen or fifteen cents from the washrags, or whether she owes it to me — and I don't know who owes who from the lemon sodas that she treated me to — but I paid for!"

Fred looked at Wilma for a moment. "I don't know who owes who what, either — but I can tell you how to handle it in the future!" he said.

"How?" asked Wilma.

"Stay away from drug stores

and washrag sales!" Fred yelled.

About an hour later the rockaphone rang. Fred answered and said, "Yeah, Barney. What's up?"

A little while later, he came into the kitchen where Wilma was doing the dishes. "Wilma," he said, "that was Barney on the phone. He needs a favor."

"What kind of favor?" said Wilma. "I'm a little suspicious about Barney and his favors!"

"Well," said Fred, "you know Betty's mother is staying with them for a couple of weeks. Now Barney tells me his brother Rodney is coming to town tomorrow to attend some kind of inventor's convention, and Barney and Betty don't have any room for him. He wants to know if we can put up Rodney in our spare room while he's at the convention."

"I was right to be suspicious," said Wilma. "The last time we did something like this for Barney, it was that great big fat Uncle Roscoe of his. Remember? The one who had such a nightmare he broke down the bed at 2 o'clock in the morning!"

"I remember," said Fred. "I never **did** get back to sleep that night! What do I tell Barney? No?"

"Oh, dear!" Wilma said. "I don't think we can do **that**. Anyhow, if we did say no, Betty'd be sure to think I was angry over the mixup today. You'd better call Barney back and tell him it's all right. But be sure to ask Barney if Rodney has nightmares!"

Fred called Barney, discovered that Rodney **never** suffered from nightmares, then told Barney that the Flintstones would make room for Rodney during the inventor's convention.

And that was the beginning of Double Rubble Trouble.

The next day was a Sunday, so Fred and Wilma were both at home with Pebbles when Barney and Betty drove up in their rockmobile with Rodney. Fred, who was reading the Sunday Bedrock Bulletin, put down the paper, looked toward the curb and said, "What in the blue blazes is THAT?"

'That' was Barney's rockmobile. Betty, Barney and Rodney were in the front seat. The back seat was full of packages, parcels, boxes and suitcases, and more were lashed to the top.

"What do you suppose all that stuff in the car and on the car is?" wondered Fred aloud.

"Maybe they're his inventions," suggested Wilma.

By this time, the three Rubbles were out of the car and coming up the walk to the front porch.

"Fred and Wilma," began Barney, "this is my brother Rodney. Rodney, this is Fred and Wilma Flintstone. You're gonna stay with them while you're attending the inventor's convention."

"Ho!" shouted Rodney. Then he shouted "Hah!" and next, as he looked around the side of the house and spied Dino ambling along, he shouted even louder, "Breadcrumbs and buttercups! Keep that — that **thing** away from me! I can't stand **any** dinosaur, much less baby ones — they make me sneeze! AaaaaCHOO!" Then he hurried to the farthest corner of the porch from where Dino was, sat down on the floor, covered his face with his hands and moaned,

"Why do these things always happen to **me**?"

Fred looked at Wilma and Wilma looked at Fred.

Barney didn't quite know what to say or do. Finally, he muttered, "Gimme a hand with the stuff from the car, Fred," and started down the front walk.

Fred caught up with him and said, "What have you gotten me into **this** time, Barney? Is he always like this?"

Barney answered gloomily, "Sometimes he's worse — but what can I do? He's my only brother! And besides, Fred, I've got a few ideas about how maybe we can make ourselves some money out of Rodney — maybe even get rich!"

By this time, they were starting to unload the car. "What the heck is **in** these boxes and car-

tons and bags and packages? Inventions?"

"I dunno," said Barney. "Maybe some of them. That big one on top I know about. That's his bed and mattress and pillows and some other stuff. A couple of cartons are filled with hot water bottles, and all kinds of medicine."

"Whaddayuh mean, his bed?" Fred yelled. "What's the matter with the one in the spare room?"

"Shhh! Not so loud — he'll hear you!" whispered Barney. "He's sensitive!"

"Aaargh!" yelled Fred. "I gotta put up with him for **how long**?"

"Just three days," answered Barney. "He's leaving as soon as the convention's over."

It took a little over an hour to unload Barney's rockmobile and carry everything inside. Then

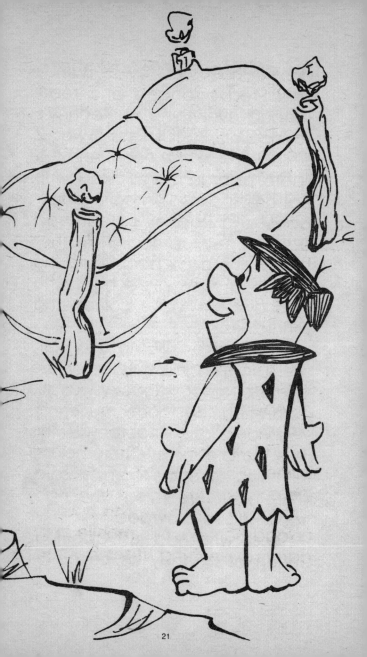

another hour went by as Barney and Fred arranged and rearranged everything to Rodney's satisfaction. By this time it was 2 o'clock in the afternoon, and the spare bedroom was filled with cartons, boxes, parcels, packages and Rodney's bed. Fred and Barney carried the other bed to the back porch, and the bathroom was piled high with Rodney's hot water bottles and medicines.

Fred, Barney, Wilma and Betty were in the hall outside of the spare bedroom. Rodney was still arranging the room, muttering, "Fishhooks and fingerbowls! This is a **terrible** mess!" Then, poking his head out of the room, he said, "Are you sure this is the right room? It's so **crowded!**"

Fred, who had just about as much of Rodney as he could

take, snapped, "You're welcome to sleep in Bedrock Park — plenty of room there!"

Barney grabbed Fred by the arm and led him down the hall to a point where Rodney couldn't hear the conversation.

"Fred," began Barney in a loud whisper, "humor him — give him whatever he wants!"

"Barney," Fred whispered, "I've put up with a lot for you — but this is the worst yet! It's not gonna take much more before I clobber him and toss him out on his ear!"

"Be patient!" hissed Barney. "I told you — I've figured out how to make money out of Rodney!"

At this point Rodney poked his head out the room again and said, "Very well. It's miserable, but I'll put up with it. Now, I de-mand absolute quiet until mid-night. Do you hear me? ABSO-LUTE QUIET! That means no chil-

dren running about, giggling and shrieking, no dinosaurs thumping around, no rockavision and no rockaphone calls! Is that clear?"

Fred was about to leap at Rodney when Barney said, "Hey, Rodney! You want it quiet so you can work on your inventions, huh?"

"No, my stupid brother," replied Rodney, "I want it quiet so I can **sleep!**"

"Sleep!" yelled Fred. "It's two o'clock in the afternoon!"

"I will explain this to you exactly once," said Rodney. "I must have absolute quiet during the day so I can sleep. At night, while **you** are asleep, I can concentrate. Which reminds me — I hope none of you snore!" Then he closed the door. The Flintstones and Rubbles could hear him through the door as he

prepared to get into bed, saying, "Mudpies and mousetraps! How can people **live** like this!"

Fred looked as if he was about to explode, but Barney stopped him with a whispered "Wait'll we get downstairs!"

When they arrived in the living room, Barney said in a low voice, "Let's drive to our house. I gotta talk to you about this whole thing!"

Ten minutes later, the two couples were in the Rubble's living room.

"Barney," said Fred, "this better be good. If Rodney gives me one more bit of lip, I'm gonna start bouncin' him off the walls!"

"Well," Barney began, "first you gotta understand something about Rodney and his inventions. He's been at it ever since he was a little boy — but the things he

invented didn't always turn out the way they were supposed to!"

"Just what the heck does **that** mean?" growled Fred. "Like what?"

"Like once I remember he invented a new kind of toothpaste," said Barney, "but it tasted terrible and made your mouth all gummy. Mom wound up using it as floor wax — she said it was the best floor wax she ever had! Then, he came up with some kind of flour and water mixture with some other stuff in it. He said it was gonna be a new and better paperclip — but any time the temperature warmed up a little, the stuff got all soggy and didn't hold its shape at all. We made macaroni out of it — pretty good macaroni, too!"

"Barney, dear," said Betty, "what I don't understand is how

you figure to make money out of Rodney's inventions when you don't know what he's invented since he was a boy — and whether whatever he's invented will work?"

"I know, I know," sighed Barney. "But the only thing I can think of is — try to make the best of it for the three days. Now, he's gonna go to the convention tomorrow. I'm taking the day off to sort of hang around with him, and while I'm with him, I'm gonna pump him to find out what kind of inventions he's invented. So that's about it, folks."

A few minutes later, Fred and Wilma went home. Wilma prepared dinner (very quietly) and after dinner they put Pebbles to bed (very, very quietly!). Not long after that, Fred whispered to Wilma, "If we can't turn on the

rockavision, we might as well go to bed, too. I have a hunch we'll need all the sleep we can get!"

At two o'clock in the morning, Fred's hunch became a reality. Wilma woke up, listened for a few moments, shook Fred and whispered, "Fred — wake up! Listen!"

"Wha — who — wassamatter?" stammered Fred, who was having a dream in which he was slowly feeding Rodney into a meatgrinder.

"Shh! Listen!" whispered Wilma.

Fred listened. He heard a loud thump, then a loud shout.

"Gadzooks and gravy! This horrible room! Can't take a step without falling over something!"

"That's Rodney!" gasped Wilma.

"Oh, puckles and pitting greens — I mean pickles and putting greens! I can't even talk straight in all this mess!"

Fred sat up in bed. "Hey!" he said, "Maybe Rodney'll get so mad he'll pack up and go home!"

"I'm afraid not," said Wilma. "It'll probably get worse!"

But the noise from Rodney's room finally stopped. Fred and Wilma gradually dropped off to sleep once more. However, at four A.M., Fred was the one who woke up this time. From Rodney's room came a tremendous shout.

"Hah-hah! Eureka! That's it! I've got it! I've got it at last! This is my best one ever!"

Wilma, who was also awake by this time, whispered, "Whatever in the world is he doing in there?"

"I think," answered Fred, "he's just invented something. And I'll tell you something else. I hope he can invent something to take the place of sleep, because from the way things are going — we're not gonna get much of it until he goes home!"

The noises from Rodney's room went on for nearly an hour. Finally, they stopped and Fred and Wilma fell asleep once more. When they awoke, Rodney was gone.

That evening, when Fred returned home from his work at the rock mine, he was so tired he was barely able to drag himself up the front walk. Wilma was waiting for him on the porch.

"Don't make any noise, dear," she said, "Rodney's sleeping. He says the convention's ruining his schedule — he has to sleep during part of his inventing time!"

"I'm too tired to make noise," replied Fred. "I'm too tired to even take a deep breath!"

A little later Wilma served dinner, and Fred fell asleep in the middle of it. At that point, the rockaphone rang. Wilma answered and then said to Fred, "It's Barney. He says he has some news. He's coming over in a few minutes."

"It'd better be quick!" moaned Fred, "because I'll be asleep in about twenty minutes — in bed, this time!"

Ten minutes later, Barney arrived and said, "Well, I was with Rodney all day. He's invented a heckava lot of things. The only trouble is, I can't see how we can make any money out of 'em!"

Wilma said, "What **are** some of Rodney's inventions, Barney? I'm curious!"

"Well, I don't think he's told me all of them — but here are the ones I got from him today. The first one is a doozy. A banana with a zipper!" said Barney.

"What's it for? What's it do?" asked Wilma.

"I dunno," replied Barney. "I guess he thinks people'll eat more bananas if they just have to pull a zipper instead of peeling them!"

"That does it!" Fred said. He was wide awake now, and getting madder by the minute. "I'm gonna go upstairs and throw Rodney, his inventions and the rest of his junk out the window!"

"Oh, be still, Fred!" said Wilma. "Tell us the rest of the inventions, Barney!"

"A gun that shoots around corners," replied Barney.

"How many corners?" asked Fred.

"How do I know?" grunted Barney. "What's the difference?"

"If it keeps on going around corners," continued Fred, "the bullet'll go right around the block and hit the shooter in the back! Hey! Maybe we can get Rodney to test it for us — that'd be **one** way of getting rid of him!"

Barney, with a disgusted look at Fred, said, "Anyhow, I can't see any way to make money out of the banana with a zipper or the gun that shoots around corners. The next one is kind of logical, in a crazy kind of way. An automobile engine that runs on ketchup instead of gasoline!"

"And you think that's logical, you meathead!" yelled Fred.

"Shhh!" whispered Wilma, "You'll wake up Rodney!"

"Oh — it's all right for dear Rodney to keep me awake all

night," snorted Fred, "but we mustn't disturb **his** beauty sleep!"

"Never mind that," said Barney. "What's wrong with the automobile engine that runs on ketchup?"

"Do you know how much ketchup COSTS?" Fred said. "About eight times as much as gasoline!"

"Yeah, stupid!" answered Barney. "But we're runnin' out of gasoline — and we've got plenty of tomatoes!"

"All right — all right!" Fred replied. "What's next on this crazy list?"

"For once in your life, you're right — this next one is **really** crazy!" Barney said. "Square tennis balls!"

"Why square ones, Barney?" Wilma asked. "What's wrong with the round ones?"

"I asked Rodney the same question," Barney said. "He said they'd stack better in the store and make tennis more interesting because of the funny bounces!"

"For once in **your** life, **you're** right!" said Fred. "We sure can't make any money out of nutty inventions like what I've heard so far!"

"Wait'll you hear the next one!" Barney said. "Dry water!"

"What is it?" asked Wilma.

"What's it look like?", asked Fred.

"What's it **for**?" asked Wilma.

"Hold it!" said Barney. "I asked him that, too! He didn't even want to talk about it. All I could get out of him was that it couldn't leak out of anything because it was dry!"

"Any more?" asked Wilma.

"Just a couple more," answered Barney. "Get a load of this: hens that lay eggs to order!"

"What's **that** mean?" Fred asked. "You just say 'egg' to a hen and she lays one?"

"Nope," said Barney. "Worse than that. You say 'fried,' or 'scrambled', or 'hard-boiled', or whatever — and that's the way they come out!"

"It'll never work, even if the hens could do it!" Fred said.

"Why not, dear?" asked Wilma. "Sounds like a great idea to me — I wouldn't have to cook your breakfast any more!"

"Here's why," Fred started to explain. "First of all, a hen only lays one egg a day. So suppose I want **two** eggs?"

Wilma said, "You'd just have more than one hen, that's all!"

"All right — suppose we had

four hens—enough for two eggs apiece every day," Fred replied. "Maybe Rodney can make 'em lay eggs fried or scrambled or boiled — but he can't **stop** 'em from laying them — and a hen lays one every day, whether you like it or not. And what kind of egg does the hen lay if you **don't** order it — the way **she** likes it best? Besides that — if a hen lays a regular egg and you don't want to use it that day, you just stick it in the refrigerator until you **do** want it! What the heck do you do with a **fried** egg you don't want, for Pete's sake? And besides **that** —"

"Sheddap!" snarled Barney. "I didn't invent it — ask Rodney!"

"Isn't there one more?" Wilma asked.

"I'm not even sure I remember what it is," Barney said slowly.

"Wait a minute — lemme think!"

"Oh, nuts!" groaned Fred. "I'm going to bed!"

"I remember," said Barney. "But like I said, it's not much."

"So what is it?" Fred said. "Hurry up!"

"Soft rocks," Barney replied.

"What do you mean, 'soft rocks', Barney?" asked Wilma. "Rocks are **supposed** to be hard. If they're soft, they're not **rocks**!"

"I told you it sounded like nothing," replied Barney. "All I know is, Rodney said something about a liquid you squirt on rocks and they go soft and powdery — almost like dust!"

"Have we heard the last of the brainstorms your nutty brother's come up with?" asked Fred, with a yawn.

"That's about it," replied Barney. "I'm going home. See you tomorrow at work. Goodnight."

"G'nite, Barney," answered Fred sleepily as he started up the steps. Suddenly Fred stopped on the steps and turned, with a strange look on his face. He came down the steps, went past a surprised Wilma and shot out of the house in a hurry. Barney was just getting into his rockmobile.

"Barney! Wait up!" called Fred.

Barney, who was behind the wheel, leaned over and watched Fred coming down the walk. "What's up?" he called as Fred neared the rockmobile.

Fred came all the way to the rockmobile, leaned in, and with a grin on his face, said, "You know something, Barney? You're even dumber than I thought you

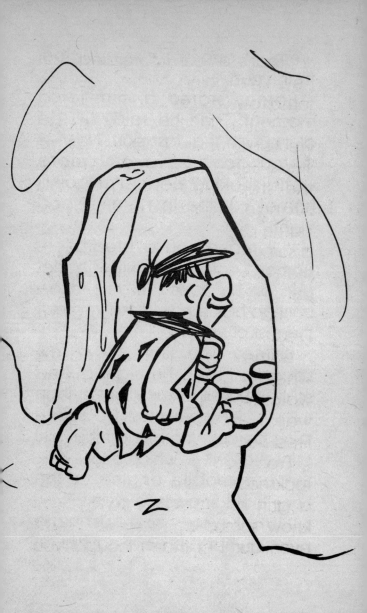

were — and I'm even dumber than you!"

Barney stared at him for a moment. Then he said, "I'll go along with that last part. Now — if you don't have any **more** world-shaking news, I'm going home! For the last time, good night!"

"I'll make you a prediction, Barney," said Fred, still with that grin on his face. "If you leave and go home now, you'll regret it the rest of your life!"

Barney was silent for a few seconds. Then he sighed and said, "I ought to know better than this — but there must be something percolating behind that silly grin! All right — which one is it — the automobile engine or the hens that lay eggs to order?"

"What you have just said proves what I've been saying for

years, Barney," said Fred. "Your brains are on a permanent vacation! Answer me a question. What do you and I do for a living — six days every week, fifty-two weeks a year?"

"I'm gonna humor you," answered Barney, "but only for one reason. The sooner I do, the sooner I get to bed. We're miners!"

"Correct!" cried Fred. "And what do we mine, Barney buddy?"

"We mine rocks! Now can I go home?" wailed Barney.

"And you **still** don't see it!" yelled Fred. "Dummy! We mine rocks! We break our backs all day clawing out those rocks — and what do we have at the end of the day?"

"Sore hands, backache, and a few rocks!" answered Barney. "So

what's new about that?"

"I'll tell you in simple words," Fred said, "because I think that thing on top of your shoulders must be one of those rocks. What was the last invention of Rodney's you told us about?"

"Lemme think," said Barney. "Oh, yeah. Soft ro —." Then he stopped.

Then he frowned. Then his face lit up and he turned to Fred with a grin as big as Fred's.

"Soft rocks," he whispered. "SOFT ROCKS!" he yelled. "Holy cow — we can mine twice as much with no effort at all!"

"**Twice** as much? **Ten** times as much!" laughed Fred.

"A hundred times as much! We'll be rich!" cried Barney.

"We'll be even richer than that! We'll find our own mine, go into business for ourselves, and put

that ugly boss of ours right out of business!" By this time Fred and Barney were yelling at the top of their lungs. Suddenly there came an interruption. An upstairs window was flung open, and Rodney's irritated voice came down to them.

"Stop that infernal yelling, you two miserable specimens! If I can't sleep—I can't invent later! Quiet!"

Fred and Barney looked at each other, and both had the same idea at the same time.

"Sorry, there, Rodney," Fred called quietly. "We were just talking about all your terrific inventions—and we got so excited I guess we forgot about you sleeping and inventing!"

"Well, just don't forget again!" Rodney snapped, and slammed down the window.

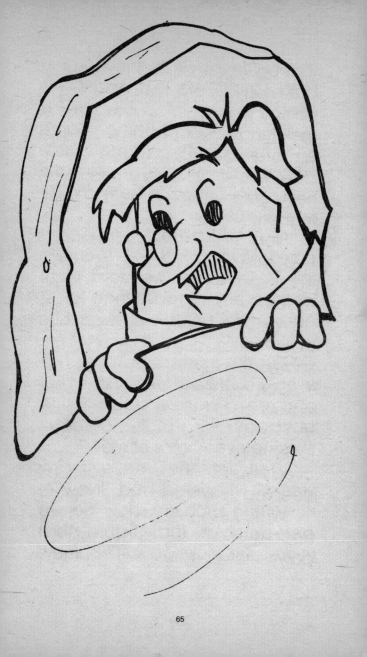

"C'mon back in the house," Fred said. "We gotta talk this over!"

When Fred and Barney came into the house, Wilma said, "What was all that noise? My stars, I thought you'd be home by now, Barney!"

Fred whispered, "Keep it down, Wilma! From now on we talk in whispers—we don't want Rodney any madder than he is! As a matter of fact, we want him to **like** us!"

"Huh!" grunted Barney. (He even whispered the grunt!) "Fat chance! Rodney doesn't like **anybody**! As a matter of fact, I think he even hates himself!"

"Well, let's not make it any worse," whispered Fred. "Now — here's the problem. How do we get hold of that liquid that makes the rocks go soft? Barney,

he's your brother. How do we do it?"

Barney started to pace up and down. "Shhhh!" whispered Fred. "Don't walk so loud!" Then Barney continued to pace, but this time on tip-toes. Finally he stopped and looked at Fred and Wilma.

"I'm not sure there **is** a way," he said. "Rodney's awfully close-mouthed about his inventions. Always was, even when he was a little kid."

"You don't think you could sweet-talk him out of it?" asked Fred.

"No way," replied Barney. "He'd figure it out in five seconds. Rodney's no dummy, even if he is a little nutty!"

"How about money—could we buy it from him?" Fred asked.

"Hard to tell," Barney answered. "I dunno whether he's

even interested in money. You see, I haven't laid eyes on him for years and years."

"Then how about this?" Fred said. "We form a company—we put up the money, and make him a partner in our rock mine. That way, he gets the money—and he can be a big shot, too — we can even make him president of the company!"

"That's probably the best idea," said Barney slowly. "But you know, Fred — two things keep bugging me. First—how much money can we get together? Neither of us has a lot of dough!"

"We'll get the money," said Fred. "Let me worry about that. We both put up as much as we can, and the Bedrock Bank will lend us the rest when I tell 'em what a good thing we've got! What's the second thing?"

"The way I see it," began Barney, "this stuff of Rodney's makes rocks crumble almost like powder. Now, that makes it easy to mine—but what about the people who want to buy rocks? They want rocks—not powder!"

"Ulp!" gasped Fred. "That's one I never thought of! And it's a bad one! Hmmm. The only thing I can think of is—you've got two jobs, now. First, find out if Rodney can do anything about the powder—and if he can, put our proposition to him and make him see it our way!"

"As usual, I get the tough job to do!" said Barney.

"You dope! If it wasn't for me, there wouldn't even **be** any kind of job to do, except tear up rocks all day long! Now, get on home, get some sleep, and go to work on Rodney tomorrow!"

"This better work out," said Barney gloomily. "I can't afford to

FOR SALE!
SOFT ROCKS

miss two day's pay and take a chance on getting fired besides!"

"Don't worry about it! Just think of all the money we'll make!" Fred said, as he shoved Barney out the front door. "Good night—and good luck tomorrow!"

Fred was sitting on the front porch steps when Barney drove up late the next afternoon. Fred came hurrying to the rockmobile. "Well?" he said, "what happened?"

"Part one is okay," said Barney. "He can make the rock powder go back into rocks. There's a lot of ingredients in the liquid that turns the rocks to powder. Call that liquid number one. All he has to do is reverse the order in which he puts 'em together and you've got liquid number two, which turns the powder back into the original rocks!"

"Yabbadabbadoo!" cried Fred. "Then all we have to do is spray liquid number one around, scoop up the powder, deliver it, and squirt liquid number two on the powder—and bing, bang, boom — we've got our rocks back! Now—what about part two—the money and the company and all that?"

"It doesn't go all that fast," said Barney. "It took me all day to get him to say he could do part one! I'm gonna have to wait until tomorrow to try it on him!"

"Think I could do any good if I came along?" asked Fred. "I could take a day off, too!"

"Don't even mention it!" replied Barney. "He thinks you're poison! Your house creaks and keeps him awake, Dino grunts in his sleep and wakes him up — he even claims he wakes up every time you slurp up a spoonful of soup!"

"Okay," answered Fred. "It's all up to you, then — but remember — tomorrow's his last day here — it's tomorrow or never!"

"I know, I know," Barney said. "I hope you don't think I'm enjoying this! I can't stand him, even if he is my brother — and he feels the same way about me! As a matter of fact, I think the only reason he was half-way polite to me today was because I tricked him into it. I flattered him every way I could think of and then said I bet he couldn't turn the rocks back into powder. He just looked at me like I was some kind of bug on the wall and then told me how he could do it!"

"So double up on the flattery tomorrow!" cried Fred. "We gotta get those two liquids! Now — go home and get a good night's sleep — tomorrow's the big day!"

"Yeah," replied Barney. "I just

hope I can pull it off! So long —
see you tomorrow!"

Fred didn't sleep much that
night. Between Rodney's loud
noises, and worrying about
whether Barney would be suc-
cessful the next day, he spent
most of the night lying in bed
wide awake.

When he awakened after a
light doze in the early morning,
Rodney was gone. And because
he knew he'd go completely
crazy if he stayed around the
house all day, he went off to
work as usual.

When he returned home, he
found Barney sitting on the front
steps, looking very, very gloomy.

Fred got out of his rockmobile,
went up the front walk and
looked closely at Barney's face.

"Well?" Fred said. "You blew
it, didn't you?"

"Nope," replied Barney.

"Then why are you looking like

a dead fish?" asked Fred. "Did he agree to do what we want?"

"Nope," replied Barney.

"Well, what happened?" yelled Fred. "Say something!"

"Okay," Barney said. "I flattered him all over the place. Had him all puffed up and primed—I thought. Then, when I put it to him, he got a happy look on his face and said he'd think about it and give us an answer when you got home. But then he said something funny. He asked me if I knew the dictionary definition of the word 'invent'. I didn't know, so that's when he said he'd tell us when you got home. But I got a bad feeling about the whole thing—when he looks happy — that means somebody else is gonna be **unhappy**."

"Rats!" cried Fred. "If he was gonna say no, he could have told you, couldn't he? Chances are he's just gonna hold out for a

bigger percentage, or some crazy conditions! I don't care — he can have whatever he wants — just so we get liquids one and two!"

Barney continued to look gloomy, but answered with a sigh, "Have it your way. Let's get it over with — go on up and talk to him."

"Cheer up!" said Fred. "A few months from now, when this thing gets going, we'll both be rolling in money! Okey-dokey—up the steps we go!"

Just then both of them heard footsteps coming down the stairs inside the house, and seconds later, Rodney came through the front door to the porch.

"Hey, there, Rodney! Come to join our party? Barney says you're all ready to join up with us and make a pile of money!" Fred cried.

Rodney just stood there, looking from one to the other. Finally, he spoke up.

"Listen very carefully," he began, "because I want you to understand exactly what I'm going to say to you. First of all, I want you to know that I would just as soon 'join up', as you put it, with a pit full of rattlesnakes, scorpions and angry bull elephants as I would you two brainless wonders! Second, brother dear, I must tell you that your behavior of the last two days has been so outrageously shameless that I had a hard time to keep from laughing right in your face at your silly, overdone flattery! The spectacle of you, Barney, who despised me just as much as I despised you, pouring out that ridiculous praise for my inventions was almost too much for me to keep a straight face!"

Here Rodney paused and looked at Fred and Barney. "Well?" he said, "nothing to say?"

When he received no answer, Rodney continued.

"Let us now take up the subject of my inventions," he said. "Since I doubt that either of you has ever **seen** a dictionary, much less read one, I will now tell you what the dictionary has to say about the word 'invent'. Are you listening? Very well. The dictionary says — at least mine does — and I have the latest — that 'invent' means 'to fabricate in the mind'. Just in case you're not familiar with 'fabricate' — **that** means 'to make'. So to invent is to make **in the mind**. The last three words are the important ones. **In the mind.** Am I clear so far?"

Fred and Barney looked at each other, and it was hard to tell which one looked more bewildered.

Then Fred said, "If I read you right through that cloud of words you just threw out, none of your inventions is real. Is that right?"

"Congratulations!" said Rodney. "I may have underestimated you. There **is** something inside of that rather unpleasant-looking lump atop your shoulders. I don't suppose one could call it a brain, but it's probably better than nothing. To answer your question, let me put it this way; there are inventors of all kinds. Most of them are dull fellows who inhabit grimy cellars or gloomy laboratories, dirtying themselves making things out of bits and pieces of junk. I, however, am a true inventor. I simply haven't the time to do the putting together. I

think things up. If someone else wants to slave away making my brain children come alive, that's their privilege. I simply can't invent and then fritter away my time bothering with testing and patching and the endless task of making things work. **My** time is too valuable for anything but thinking up wonderful new ideas!"

"Like square tennis balls," said Barney.

"And bananas with zippers," said Fred.

"Exactly!" exclaimed Rodney. "Aren't they terrific inventions?"

"I'll tell you," said Fred. "I have an invention of my own. I just invented it. I'm not gonna tell you what it is — but if you're not packed and out of here in nine minutes, my invention is gonna leave you scattered in a million pieces between here and the railroad station!"

"Funny," said Barney. "I just invented the same thing!"

Nine minutes later, Rodney was packed and gone.

After a long silence, Barney got up from the front steps and started down the walk to his rockmobile. When he got there, he turned and called to Fred, "Speaking of inventions—"

"Don't," replied Fred, "or I'll invent a new way of separating you from your head!"

"I need one," said Barney. "In fact, I need two of 'em!"

"Get it off your chest," growled Fred.

"The first one," said Barney, "is a way to keep my job at the mine after taking three days off without even telling the boss."

"What's number two?" Fred asked.

"A way to keep Betty from killing me for losing three day's pay

without even telling **her**!" Barney
replied.

"You think **you** got trouble?"
Fred grunted. "I lost three nights
sleep, worked my fingers to the
bone all day, had to put up with
your charming brother, and now
— I'm gonna hafta listen to
Wilma telling me 'I **told** you so!'
for the next six months!"

"G'nite, Fred," said Barney.

"G'nite, Barney," said Fred.

And that was the sad end of
Double Rubble Trouble!